Treasury of
Fairy
Tales

Treasury of Fairy Tales

MODERN PUBLISHING
A Division of Unisystems, Inc.
New York, NY 10022

Published by Modern Publishing
A Division of Unisystems, Inc.

Originally published as Contes du temps passé by
Éditions Lito - Paris
© Lito Éditrice - Milan

CONTENTS

Sleeping Beauty

by Charles Perrault

Once upon a time in a land far away, there lived a king and queen whose dearest wish in all the world was to have a child of their very own.

They hoped and prayed so strongly that one day their wish came true.

A beautiful baby girl was born to them. Her hair was the color of spun gold and her eyes were as blue as the bluest summer sky.

The joy of the king and queen was indescribable. The little princess captured the heart of the whole court.

Preparations were made for her christening and great celebrations were organized throughout the land.

The king invited the seven fairies who lived in his realm to be godmothers to his daughter. Then they could watch over the princess's happiness and help her to grow in beauty and in wisdom.

The seven fairies accepted this invitation with pleasure. On the day of the christening, they came to the castle to present their gifts to their goddaughter.

A great banquet had been prepared in their honor. After the ceremony, they all sat down at the table.

Suddenly an old fairy arrived whom nobody had thought to invite because she hadn't set foot outside her door for more than fifty years. Everyone thought she must have died and they had forgotten all about her.

The king apologized most profusely for this oversight and kindly invited her to join the festivities.

But the old fairy, who was very touchy, thought that she had been scorned and was outraged.

She sat at the table, but didn't stop muttering under her breath until the end of the meal.

After the banquet, the fairies gathered around the cradle of the little princess and started to present their gifts.

The first one promised her beauty, the second intelligence, the third one grace. The others promised her great talents for dancing, singing and music.

Suddenly, the old fairy leaned over the baby.

"This child will be happy and clever," she said, "but one day she will prick her finger on a spindle and die!"

When the princess's parents and godmothers heard this terrible curse, they despaired.

Happily, one of them had not yet made her promise to the princess. She quickly declared:

"Take comfort, your Majesties, your princess will not die. I can not undo the spell completely. The child *will* prick her finger, but she will fall into a deep sleep that will last a

hundred years, until the day a prince comes to wake her."

Immediately, the king took measures to avoid the old fairy's curse. He published an edict throughout the land forbidding the spinning of wool, and all spinning wheels and spindles were publicly burned.

The king and queen were very anxious, but as time went by, they took heart and hoped that their little princess might be spared from such an unhappy fate as the old fairy foretold.

The child was growing prettier each day. Her sweetness and the kindness of her character made her beloved of everyone who knew her.

The fairies, who were looking after her education, were very proud of their pupil.

The princess was approaching her sixteenth birthday when, one day, running around the castle and exploring all its nooks and crannies, she climbed to the top of an old tower.

At the top of the stairs was a little door. She opened it and entered a dark and musty room. In the middle of the room, she noticed a spindle. Since she had never seen such a thing before and knew nothing of the old fairy's prophecy, she went up and touched the strange object curiously.

She pricked her finger and fainted, falling into a deep sleep.

When they found the princess lying unconscious on the floor, the good fairies decided to cast a spell of their own, sending *everyone* in the castle to sleep. So, when the princess woke in a hundred years, she wouldn't be alone in the old castle.

At the wave of a magic wand, everyone fell fast asleep in the middle of whatever they were doing.

One day, a hundred years later, a prince, who was hunting thereabouts, was intrigued to see the towers of a distant castle rising above the forest.

An old man told him the legend of the beautiful sleeping princess and, in a flash, he knew that he was the prince who would free her from her prison of slumber.

Without wasting a minute, he set off with a heart full of hope and impatience.

On the way, he met an old hermit who told him how to reach the bewitched castle.

The prince thanked the hermit and plunged into the dense forest that surrounded the building.

Thorns, tangled trees and bushes barred his way. It seemed hopeless. But suddenly, as if by magic, a path opened up before him.

Bolts of lightning flashed across the black sky, and raging thunder shook the trees in the forest. Undaunted, the brave prince drew nearer to the castle.

He arrived at the gates, where he saw the guards snoring in their sentry boxes. In the courtyard, an even more curious spectacle awaited him: animals, servants, cooks and valets, all appeared to have fallen asleep, quite suddenly, in mid-step or in mid-sentence. It seemed as though time had stood still for this enchanted castle.

The young man crossed several rooms, all full of sleeping people, before he reached the princess's chamber.

When he saw her lying there, his heart swelled with love. In all his life he had never seen such a beautiful princess.

Even asleep, she shone more brightly than any star. He knelt beside her and placed a tender kiss on her forehead.

As the fairy had predicted, the spell was broken. The princess opened her eyes and looked at the prince who was still gazing at her in mute admiration.

"Is it you, my prince? You've certainly taken your time!" she said.

The prince was charmed by her wit and lost no time in telling her that he loved her with all his heart.

Meanwhile, everyone in the castle had awakened and was carrying on with the activities interrupted a hundred years before.

The prince and the princess decided to be married as soon as possible.

It was not long before the whole country was celebrating their wedding. The festivities went on for several weeks because, after sleeping for such a long time, everyone was full of energy and gaiety.

As for the prince and princess, they had a son and a daughter of their own and lived happily ever after.

The Griffin

by the Brothers Grimm

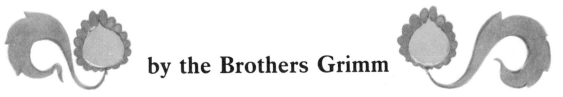

In a far distant country, lived a very rich king who had only one daughter.

The princess was very beautiful but, sadly, she suffered from an incurable illness that had kept her confined to her bed for many years.

Well-known doctors of many lands tried to cure her but none succeeded.

One fine day, a fairy arrived in the land and asked to speak to the king.

"To cure the princess," she revealed in a mysterious voice, "you need an apple!"

The very next morning, with great beating of drums and blowing of trumpets, the heralds of the court proclaimed a royal edict.

"By order of the king, the man who brings to the court the magical apple which has the power to cure the princess, will be granted the honor of her hand in marriage!"

John, a young peasant boy who lived on a nearby farm, had as his only possession a tree that produced the roundest, reddest, juiciest apples in the world.

When he heard about the king's edict, John filled a basket to the brim with his apples and set out for the palace.

A little way down the road, he met a dwarf with a wrinkled face, and a long white beard.

"What do you have in that basket?" asked the little man.

"These are the apples that are going to cure the princess!"

"Well then, so be it!" replied the dwarf and disappeared.

As soon as he arrived at the palace, the young peasant boy had the basket of apples taken to the king's daughter.

The princess received the present with joy and, choosing one of the apples, started to eat it hungrily.

She had hardly swallowed the last mouthful when magically she leaped out of bed, completely cured.

At first, the relief and happiness of the king and the court dignitaries knew no bounds, but when the first flush of enthusiasm had passed, the king began to regret that he had so hastily promised his daughter's hand to a simple peasant.

So he said to the young man,

"If you wish to take the princess, my daughter, for your wife, you must take these hundred rabbits out to pasture and bring them all back at the end of the day. Otherwise you must give up the idea of marrying the princess."

Being a courageous lad, John agreed to this test.

The next day, he set off early in the morning with the hundred white rabbits, but as soon as he reached the field they scampered off in a hundred different directions.

The young man was in despair. How was he going to be able to take them all back to the palace that evening? Suddenly, the dwarf with the long white beard appeared, and John was very happy to see him again. The dwarf gave him a small magic whistle.

He put it to his lips and all the rabbits reappeared and ran to sit at his feet.

As dusk fell, a very disgruntled king saw the young man return with every single one of the hundred rabbits.

Nevertheless, he said to the young peasant,

"You can marry my daughter, but only on one condition. You must build a boat that can sail over land as well as over water!"

John walked back to his village racking his brain to figure out how he could possibly satisfy the absurd demand of his king. But once again, taking his courage in both hands, he set himself resolutely to the task.

He had already been working for quite a while, and the boat was beginning to take shape, when the dwarf with the long white beard appeared once more. The little man watched John work in silence. Then, after a moment, he said,

"You seem to have taken on quite a task there, my boy! Do

you think you'll be able to do it? And, by the way, what exactly is it that you're trying to build?"

"The king has commanded me to build a boat that can sail over land as well as water."

The dwarf said nothing at first, then, as he had at their previous meetings, he said the magic words:

"Well then, so be it!"

And he disappeared as suddenly as he had come, as silent as a shadow.

For long days and nights, John worked tirelessly to complete his project. When the boat was finished, he climbed into it, hardly daring to hope . . . .

Imagine his amazement when he found that the magical boat slipped as easily across fields and along roads, as it did on the river!

Happier than ever, the young man went whistling on his

way to the palace and requested an audience with the king.

To the utter astonishment of the whole court, John demonstrated what his extraordinary boat could do. The magic vessel sailed along the pathways of the park as smoothly as it did on the calm waters of the lake.

The king took possession of the boat, which was everything that he had imagined it would be. But, once again, he did not keep the promise he had made.

"This is all very well!" he said. "But it is not enough. If you want to marry the princess, my daughter, you must bring me one of the griffin's feathers!"

A shocked gasp ran through the assembled company, because everyone knew that the griffin was a legendary animal that was almost impossible to approach since it hated all men. Being half eagle and half lion, its appearance was extraordinary. It lived in a remote corner of the world, safe from intruders. Nobody had ever even been near enough to it to actually catch sight of it!

It was with a heavy heart indeed that John left the court. He trudged slowly towards his home, lost in thought.

"Perhaps this task is the last one the king will demand of me. But it's an impossible one, all the same!"

Just then, the dwarf with the long white beard sprang up beside him. When he showed him the road that led to the

place where the monstrous bird lived, the young man's sadness flew away at once.

After he had traveled for many days and many weeks and crossed the borders of many lands, wearily John finally reached the griffin's lair. But the strange bird was not there.

Instead, John was met by the fairy Gelsomine who told him that she was the guardian of the lair. She knew the griffin better than anyone in the world, because she had looked after it when it was a baby.

Gelsomine was a very kind-hearted fairy, and she made the young man welcome. She listened attentively to the story of his adventures, which he told her from the very beginning.

When he had finished, she looked at him pityingly,

"I must tell you," she started by warning him, "that the griffin is the most ill-tempered bird in the world. It really hates men and devours any that it comes across! But I can see that you are a brave boy and that you're not afraid, so I am going to help you."

The fairy beckoned the young man into her house and, motioning him to follow her, led him down strange, gloomy stairs that went deep underground. Wide-eyed John gazed about him, intrigued to discover the mysterious haunt of the fairy and of the bird.

It was like nothing that John had ever seen before. It was a staircase-filled labyrinth, with corridor after corridor leading into each other as far as the eye could see. At the end of a last passageway, they saw the light of day once more.

The fairy Gelsomine stopped there. Then, turning to look at John, she quickly measured him with her eyes and, pointing towards a hole cut into the wall, said to him,

"That hiding place is rather narrow, but you're slim, I think it will be big enough for you. Hide in there and when the griffin comes back, you'll be able to see it without it seeing you. Watch what it does. As soon as you're sure that it's sound asleep, you can creep up and pluck one of its feathers."

Night was falling and still John waited for the griffin's return. Suddenly a huge shadow blotted out the entrace to the tunnel: the legendary bird had come home.

"I smell human flesh!" the griffin thundered angrily.

"Yes, you probably do" replied the fairy. "A traveler who had lost his way stopped to ask directions, but he's gone now."

Her explanation seemed to convince the griffin who then fell into a deep sleep.

Moments later, John crept up on tiptoe to stand beside the awesome sleeping bird. Mustering up all his courage, he quickly plucked out a feather.

His task safely completed, he stopped to thank the good fairy Gelsomine who had been so kind to him. Then, with a spring in his step and new hope in his heart, the young man set out on his journey home.

He arrived at the palace in triumph. John brandished the griffin's feather aloft, and the whole court cheered him. This time, the king proved incapable of dreaming up any more excuses to delay the wedding.

And, at the bottom of his heart, the king was congratulating himself for having found his daughter a husband who had proved himself to be so good and so courageous. The king was convinced that such a man could make his beloved

daughter happy. The young couple, who really hardly knew each other, were so delighted at the announcement of their marriage that they absolutely insisted that the wedding be held the very same day.

The king gave a great banquet at the palace, and all the people of the land came to stand and cheer. Then, the king opened the ball by dancing with the princess. Afterwards the newlyweds, who were already very much in love, danced the night away in each other's arms.

Never was there a happier royal couple. Many years later, people still talked about the valiant man who, in his youth, had so bravely won the hand of his princess.

Prince Charming

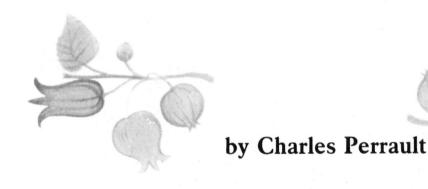

by Charles Perrault

Once upon a time there was a king who was so good and so generous that his subjects called him "Heart of Gold."

One day, while he was walking through the woods, a wild rabbit that was being chased by hunters suddenly jumped into his arms for refuge.

The king comforted the poor trembling thing, took it back to the palace and sent for some lettuce to feed it.

No sooner had the animal eaten its fill when, all at once, it turned into one of the most beautiful ladies that the king had ever seen!

"I am the White Fairy," she said to the king who was gazing at her in wonder. "I turned myself into a rabbit to test your kindness. I see now how great it is! In return, I will grant all your desires. Just tell me what you wish."

"Oh, lovely fairy," replied the king, "all I wish for is that my son, Prince Charming, should be the gentlest and the most just king in the world."

"I will do my best to help you," promised the fairy, and then she disappeared into thin air.

A few months later, the old king Heart of Gold died.

Prince Charming succeeded his father to the throne and started to reign with justice and generosity.

One day, the White Fairy appeared to him. She urged him to stay as good and wise as he was and gave him a magic ring.

"Remember!" she warned him. "If ever you commit a dishonest act, the ring will prick your finger. It will be a warning to you to guard against falling into evil ways."

Alas! The new king was very young and very inexperienced. Before long, he was surrounded by a number of

wicked courtiers. They were a very bad influence on him and led him into many unjust decisions and actions.

Gradually, almost without being aware of it, Prince Charming became a cruel and violent king, ill-tempered and tyrannical.

The magic ring that the good fairy had given him pricked his finger in vain: he simply ignored it.

One summer day, a big hunting party had been organized. Charming had wandered away from his companions and as he walked down a forest path, he met a little shepherdess who answered to the sweet name of Celia. The young man fell so madly in love at the sight of her that he asked her to marry him.

But Celia had heard about the king's bad reputation and refused to be married to someone so evil. Charming, furious at being rejected, had the shepherdess taken to his palace.

But, when he wanted to go and see his prisoner, he learned that she had escaped.

His wicked courtiers told him that his old tutor Soliman had helped her run away.

Blinded with rage, Charming ordered that his faithful old servant be locked up in the deepest and darkest dungeon in the castle.

This unjust sentence had hardly left his lips when the whole castle was rocked by a deafening clap of thunder. In that very instant, Charming found himself in the heart of the

forest, transformed into a hideous animal. His evil ways had turned him into a monster!

Driven half mad, he started to run hither and thither, roaring and grunting like a wild animal, until he fell into a trap laid by the huntsmen.

It was there that he was found by the director of a circus, who decided that this monster would make a fine new attraction in the big ring.

Not recognized as the king, Charming was locked in a cage with the lions and tigers.

He patiently bore constant whippings and humiliations. He began to realize the evil of his ways and was sincerely repentant.

The memory of the pretty shepherdess was with him

always. He wished with all his heart that he could win her love.

One day, one of the tigers attacked their trainer. Charming leaped at the ferocious beast and saved the life of his tormentor. In that instant, he heard a sweet voice say,

"Every good deed deserves its reward!"

And in a flash he was turned into a little dog. So a new life was starting for the young man, but it was not to be much happier than the last.

Indeed, his masters hardly gave him anything to eat and he was often starving

One day as he was roaming the streets of the town, having just unearthed a nice fresh piece of bread, he caught sight of a poor beggar girl with a pale face who looked hungry.

Full of pity, the little dog trotted up to her and gave her his only possession: his one and only meal of the day.

In that second, he heard a sweet voice say,

"Every good deed deserves its reward!"

And in a flash, the little dog was transformed into a beautiful bird of paradise with multicolored plumage and flew up high into the sky, twittering with joy.

Charming was filled with gratitude and hope. Now his dearest desire was to find Celia again.

He set out immediately to look for her.

He flew for days on end and searched the kingdom from top to bottom.

Asking directions from the animals of the plains and the forests, he finally reached a steep mountain.

There he found a grotto, the home of an old hermit. Then

he saw the young shepherdess sitting next to the old man.

His heart was beating as if it would burst out of his little bird's body.

But he realized the great distance that still separated them. She would not recognize him . . . he was just a bird . . . . He flew to Celia's shoulder and, enchanted by his beauty, she stroked him gently.

Charming was restored to human form, while the White Fairy appeared in place of the old man. True love had broken the spell.

With the good fairy's help, Celia and Prince Charming returned to the palace. There, they found Soliman who had been freed by the people and elected to rule in place of the cruel vanished king.

Soliman had reigned with wisdom, knowing that one day his master would return. He was overjoyed to see the young king transformed by love and handed him the crown with tears in his eyes.

The wedding took place a few days later amid great celebrations which were conducted throughout the land.

From that day on, Charming reigned with wisdom and justice, more than fulfilling his father's dearest wish.

The Little Match Girl

by Hans Christian Andersen

Long ago, in a big town in Denmark, there lived a sweet and charming, but very poor little girl.

She lived in an icy garret with her father, a detestable man who didn't look after her and even beat her when she didn't bring home enough money.

The poor child had no one in the world to protect her. She had lost her mother when she was young, and her grandmother who had been so good to her had died a few months earlier, leaving her quite helplessly alone.

To earn enough money to live on, the little girl had to go out every day into the streets of the town to sell boxes of matches to passers-by. But even this was becoming more and more difficult.

It was New Year's Eve.

The weather was very cold, and thick snowflakes were blanketing the ground.

Snug and warm in their houses, children were playing with the toys that their parents had given them for Christmas. The few people who ventured out in spite of the biting cold, all walked along as briskly as they could, hurrying back to the comfort of their homes.

Only the little match girl wandered through the town, from one street to another. Shivering as she walked on the snow in her bare numbed feet, she clutched her most precious possession, the cardboard box that held her matches, under her arm.

When she had left home that morning, she had been wearing a pair of old slippers that had belonged to her grandmother. But they were so big that she had lost them

running to get out of the way of the big cars of the wealthy shoppers.

Finally, the little girl stood still. Her teeth were chattering with cold!

It was getting dark . . . no use going any farther!

She sat down and curled up in a corner between two houses. She thought sadly about her mother, her dear, kind, gentle mother, whom she remembered only dimly, but with a great deal of love.

It had been so many years since her mother had died that the poor child could hardly remember her face. Her only memory was of the sweetness with which she would take her in her arms to rock her gently or to tell her a story.

If only she were still alive!

She was getting colder and colder by the minute. Her little hands were numb and her eyes filled with tears as she looked anxiously at the boxes of matches that she still hadn't sold. From time to time, she got up and tried to get warm by moving around.

Suddenly, she had an idea! Perhaps, if she were to light a match, it would give enough heat to warm her fingers which were now blue, and as stiff as little icicles.

Oh! If only she dared!

She could light just one so that her father wouldn't suspect anything. But what if he found out? . . . Wondering how he possibly could she summoned her courage.

With a trembling hand, she took one match out of the box, looked at it for a long time and then rubbed it against the wall. A bright warm flame sprang up and shone in the dark night.

But what could that strange light be?

It seemed to the little girl as though she were sitting next to a big stove. She could actually see its shiny copper lid.

The fire inside was crackling and burning brightly. Oh, how lovely and warm it was!

She was stretching out her hands to warm them at the fire, when the flame went out, the stove disappeared and she found herself huddled in her corner again, with a burned-out match between her fingers.

Undaunted, she picked out another match and rubbed it quickly against the wall.

In its pale glow, the wall behind her was suddenly as transparent as glass: the child saw a beautiful room with a richly laid table standing in the center.

The crystal glasses and porcelain plates sparkled on the damask tablecloth. In the middle of the table was a big, fat roasted goose that smelled absolutely delicious.

Suddenly, the goose seemed to roll off the platter, off the table and across the floor towards the little girl, as if to offer itself to her.

Quickly, the little match girl reached out towards the food, but the match went out and the roast goose disappeared . . . . There was nothing in front of her but a cold hard wall!

A third match burst into flame and, all at once, the little girl found herself kneeling at the foot of a magnificent Christmas tree.

It was taller and more beautiful than any she had ever seen, even those in the grand houses she'd peeped into.

Thousands of candles burned brightly on its green branches. Threads of gold and silver, shining glass balls and multicolored stars twinkled and sparkled as she watched with eyes full of wonder.

Her arms reached out, but the flame of the match died, as the Christmas candles rose higher and higher. Soon they were stars shining up above, lighting the dark, winter night sky.

At that very moment, a shooting star drew a dazzling furrow across the heavens as it fell.

"Someone is dying," thought the little girl as she

remembered what her grandmother always used to say:

"A shooting star is a soul that is flying to God!"

She rubbed another match against the wall. She saw her grandmother surrounded by a shimmering halo, smiling at her lovingly.

"Grandmother!" she cried, bursting into tears. "Take me with you, please! I'm so afraid that you will disappear like the stove, the goose, and the tree when this match goes out!"

As fast as she could, the little girl lit all the matches that were left in the box. They burned with a radiant light.

Her grandmother was still smiling, more beautiful than she had ever been. Then she reached for the child, lifted her gently up into her arms and, together, bathed in a golden glow, they flew higher and higher . . . to where there was no cold, no hunger and no sadness . . . .

Next morning, the townspeople found the poor little girl's body in the corner between the houses.

"She must have been trying to get warm, poor little thing," said a passer-by, and hurried on.

And no one would ever know the wonderful things that the little match girl had seen or the infinite joy she had found, with her grandmother, on that New Year's Day.

The Little Myrtle Fairy

by Giambattista Basile

 Florence was a good, kind woman who lived in a little cottage on the edge of the forest. She had lived alone for many years and her solitude weighed heavily upon her.

"If only I had a child to keep me company," she often used to sigh. "A little girl I could teach to knit and cook. She could come into the garden with me, pick flowers to make bouquets, and we could sing songs together. My life would be so much happier, and the winters wouldn't seem so very long!"

One evening, while Florence was sitting by the side of the hearth thinking these sad thoughts, she suddenly had an idea.

"What if I were to go to the enchanted wood to look for the fairy that the old folk still whisper about. The one who lives under the oldest oak tree in the forest – the fairy Graciosa. They say that she is compassionate and generous in her gifts."

Ferdinand the cat and Biscuit the dog tried hard to make her change her mind, one by purring and the other by whimpering (because they were very jealous), but Florence, undeterred, set out along the path that led to the forest.

But how disappointed she was! The fairy Graciosa was very old, and her magic powers had waned with age. Nevertheless, she gave the startled woman a present of a pretty little plant in a pot.

"Take good care of it," she told Florence. "It will bring happiness into your house."

That very evening, Florence put the myrtle plant (for that is what it was) on her window sill. With careful watering, it grew stronger every day, but Florence was still alone.

One day, the king's son happened to pass by. Intrigued, he asked,

"Where does that strange plant come from? I have never seen the like of it before. To tell the truth, I like it very much and if you would be so kind as to give it to me, I promise to take great care of it, and in return, to pay you generously for it."

Florence was poor, so very poor! She thought that the fairy's prediction was about to come true, because at last fortune was smiling upon her. So she sold the plant. With heavy heart, she watched the prince vanish in the distance, clutching the precious little plant under his cape.

Soon afterwards, Florence, now a wealthy woman, married a prosperous farmer, a widower with many children. The fairy's prophecy had been fulfilled and Florence often

thought with emotion and gratitude of the little plant.

Meanwhile, the myrtle plant had pride of place in the royal greenhouse. It grew taller and more beautiful with each day that went by.

The prince and his courtiers came to see it very often and each time he appeared, the slender twigs bowed to him, the new leaves quivered and rustled.

The young prince was surprised and, sensing that some magic was at work here, he decided to install the plant on the terrace of his private apartments, so that he could take care of it himself. Henceforth, he alone watered it and took great care, each morning, to turn the pot so that the myrtle plant could bask in the rising sun.

One fine morning in May, the prince found a beautiful young girl standing by the plant. The gold of her hair, the

rosy hue of her delicate complexion, together with her grace and beauty, captured the young man's heart in an instant.

'Who are you, beautiful vision?" he asked with bated breath.

"Fleur de Lys, sire, princess of the myrtles," the lovely stranger replied. "To save me from the wrath of a wicked wizard, the fairy Graciosa, my godmother, made me very, very small and hid me for a long time in the middle of the plant. Thanks to your tender care, I am now returned to my normal size. How can I ever thank you?"

"Why, by marrying me, beautiful Fleur de Lys!" cried the delighted prince.

As he was handsome, kind and brave, the young woman eagerly accepted his proposal.

Months went by, there was no cloud to mar the happiness

of the newlyweds. Then the wicked Lord of the Five Rivers declared war on the prince. The thought of leaving his sweet bride distressed him greatly, but Fleur de Lys said to him,

"Go, my husband, your first duty is to safeguard your kingdom. To await your return in all safety, I shall return to my hiding place inside the plant.

When you come back from battle, ring the little silver bell that I shall hang on the lowest twig. Then, and only then, shall I reappear."

The prince knew how jealous the ladies of the court were of his pretty wife and how many of them wished her ill, so he was relieved to see her disappear into the foliage. He entrusted the precious myrtle plant to a faithful servant.

"You are to let no one come near the pot," he warned the valet. "You will answer for it with your life."

He left with an easy mind, spreading the rumor that his wife had entered a convent for the period of his absence.

But two particularly malicious ladies-in-waiting had overheard the prince's conversation with his wife. They immediately decided to take their revenge.

The poor valet was given a drugged cup of wine to drink, and while he slept, the two wicked women savagely stamped the fragile myrtle plant into the ground, after they had rung the precious little bell.

When the valet regained consciousness, he found a lock of golden hair among the broken stems on the ground by the pot. Horrified and terror-struck, he took flight before the return of his master, whose just anger he dared not face!

When the prince returned, victorious, from war, all he

found on the deserted terrace were a few withered branches hung with dried leaves and, nearby, a tarnished silver bell.

The young man wept as he rang and rang the little bell, but it was in vain: no answer came. Fleur de Lys was lost.

The poor brokenhearted prince cloistered himself inside his castle, banishing all his courtiers and their wives. In the deserted palace, his footsteps echoed as he paced up and down the corridors. The shivering servants hurried to the kitchens. At least there was a bit of warmth by the fire!

Finally, one May morning, the prince roused himself from his melancholy and wanted to see his dear myrtle plant again. He went out onto the terrace and to his surprise and joy he found the plant green again and in full flower! Cautiously, with the tips of his fingers, he rang the little bell. A shimmering mist floated down and, when it cleared, there was Fleur de Lys smiling at her husband!

"My dearest husband," said the young woman in her sweet melodious voice, "your faithfulness has been rewarded, for this plant is the symbol of lovers who cannot be parted. We shall be happy together now and forever."

The prince punished the ladies-in-waiting severely and ordered great festivities to celebrate the return of his beloved wife.

For days on end, there was dancing in the castle, in the streets, and in the fields. And while the people of the kingdom rejoiced in their princess, a good farmer's wife danced with her children and, in her heart, gratefully thanked "the little myrtle fairy."

The Water of Life

by the Brothers Grimm

Long ago, there reigned a king who was beloved of all his subjects for his wisdom and his goodness. His wife was as generous as she was beautiful. She had meals distributed to the beggars and made sure herself that wholesome food was fairly shared between them. The royal couple had three sons. The kingdom prospered and everyone in the land was grateful that they were blessed with such a good and fine monarch to reign over them.

Alas! One sad day the king fell gravely ill. Famous doctors, magicians and all manner of wise men were called to his bedside. Prayers were offered up and in churches throughout the land people gathered to plead for heaven's mercy.

But, in spite of all their efforts and prayers, the state of the king's health just went from bad to worse. An old soothsayer looked into his crystal ball, but it remained obstinately clouded and refused to reveal the future.

"Bad sign, very bad," muttered the old man, while the doctors bustled around the royal bed.

"Toad's spit and spider's web," one of them declared. "That's the only remedy!"

And he shook his white head as he closed his book of spells.

"What twaddle!" exclaimed another. "I tell you, what we need are leeches. Modern remedies are the best!"

The queen, tired of listening helplessly to their endless arguments, summoned her three sons.

"Scour the country, search every village and hamlet. I am certain that you will find some wise old man who can help us to cure your father. All these bickering doctors are only

making him worse. Go, my children, and God speed!"

The three boys saddled their horses and rode off at once.

A few days later, a litter stopped in front of the palace steps and out of it, supported by the three princes, stepped a very old man. He was taken straight to the royal bedchamber where he examined the king.

"Your father's condition is very serious indeed. There is only one remedy that can save him. He must drink of the Water of Life. I can tell you no more because one of you will have to bring it to him and it will not be easy to find. But the more difficult the search, the more effective the remedy."

The hastily convened Council of Ministers was entrusted with the governing of the kingdom in the absence of the princes. Then the three brothers separated, having decided that they would each try their luck by setting off in different directions.

The eldest had been riding along for many hours under a blazing sun, when a dwarf leaped out from behind a hedge.

"Gentle sir, where are you bound?" asked the little man in a friendly tone.

"Get out of my way," growled the prince, "or my horse will smash all your miserable bones."

And he galloped off in a cloud of dust. Soon he rode his horse into a narrow gorge between two rocky mountains. To his untold horror, the walls of the mountain closed around him, locking him fast as surely as the walls of any prison.

Meanwhile, the second prince had arrived in the valley. His horse reared, as, once again, the dwarf jumped out of the bushes.

"Where are you bound, my prince?" asked the friendly little man again.

"Out of my way, you ugly gnome!" shouted the young man and spurred his horse on.

An hour later, he too found himself held prisoner.

The youngest of the princes arrived in the lost valley a few minutes before sunset.

"Why are you in such a hurry, young sir?" asked the mysterious little man once more.

"Alas, my father is dying!" the young man replied sadly. "I have to find a flask of the Water of Life, and as quickly as I can. It is the only hope we have of saving him!"

"That is indeed a commendable task," said the dwarf. "I am going to help you. The magical water spills from a fountain in the courtyard of a castle. Ride up the mountain path that you can see just beyond the trees. Do not be afraid,

you will be in no danger, and on the other side of the wild mountain stands the enchanted castle.

Knock at the door and say these words:

"The Water of Life as it spills will cure my father of his ills."

The prince thanked the dwarf warmly and spurred his horse at a gallop toward the mountain. He reached the top without mishap and soon caught sight of the castle ramparts.

The drawbridge lowered and the great studded door opened smoothly before him when he had spoken the magic words. Dismounting, he left his horse in the courtyard of the castle, then crossed several magnificently decorated, but deserted, rooms. He eventually reached the throne room and stopped in his tracks with amazement.

A young girl, a vision of sheer beauty, was seated gracefully on the sumptuous throne, her head resting on her shoulder, fast asleep. When the prince knelt at her feet, she stretched lazily, opened her eyes and smiled at her admirer.

"Thanks to you, the spell is broken," she said. "Make a wish and I will do my best to grant it."

"Beautiful maiden," said the prince, "one wish springs to my lips and that is to have you for my bride. But first of all, I have to fill a flask with the Water of Life, which my dying father most urgently needs. A kind dwarf told me that the fountain in this castle runs with this miraculous water."

"Follow me," said the princess. "The dwarf was right."

And, picking up a flask, she led him to a pool that flowed with the fresh water of a fountain. Once the flask was filled the young people exchanged tender farewells.

"In a year, I shall return to marry you," promised the prince as he leaped into the saddle.

The dwarf was waiting for him at the bottom of the mountain.

"I beg of you, kind sir," pleaded the prince, "tell me where to find my brothers. I cannot abandon them like this."

The dwarf was swayed by the young man's entreaties and freed the two arrogant princes. But, before they parted company, he warned the young prince to beware of his crafty brothers.

The three boys returned to the palace of the king, their father, in triumph. On the way, the two elder princes had stolen the flask of the Water of Life. They replaced it with water from the river, and therefore the promised remedy had no effect at all. Amid general consternation, the treacherous princes produced the real Water of Life.

In sugary tones, they said to their father, now most happily cured,

"Sire, we wanted to be fair and give our young brother his chance too, but we were the ones who braved a thousand dangers and fought the dragons that guard the Water of Life, so that you would be cured!"

Their lies were so convincing that the king believed them and exiled his youngest son. The prince went back to the enchanted castle where the princess awaited him, and married her. So he became the king of a prosperous land.

His gloating brothers became so arrogant and hateful that the king, recognizing them for what they were, disowned them both and was reconciled with his loyal and valiant youngest son.

Thumbelina

by Hans Christian Andersen

Once upon a time there was a young woman who wished more than anything for a daughter to love.

At her wits' end, she went to see a famous old witch and begged her for her help to get a little girl of her own.

"That shouldn't be too difficult," the old witch replied. "Here's a barley corn. It's not the ordinary sort, mind you, that grows in the fields or is fed to the chickens. Plant it in a pot and wait patiently for it to grow. You will be very pleasantly surprised."

The young woman thanked the old witch gratefully, gave her a few coins for her trouble and, clutching the barley corn tightly in her hand, went home.

She was terribly impatient for the corn to sprout, and sat staring at it every morning, willing it to grow.

Then one morning, she saw a little flower in bud, that looked rather like a tulip, poking out of the soil.

"Oh, what a lovely flower!" she cried with delight, brushing it with her lips.

At once, as if by magic, the petals opened and there, at the very center of the petals, was a little girl no taller than a thumb. She was so sweet that the young woman christened her Thumbelina.

The new mother happily made Thumbelina's bed out of a polished nut shell. She gathered pollen to make a mattress and covered it with sheets made out of rose petals.

So that Thumbelina would have something to amuse her, her mother had put a plate full of water on the table, with a leaf floating in it. The little girl could now sail happily round and round, and never tire of doing so.

One night, when Thumbelina was fast asleep in her nutshell bed, a big toad hopped in the open window and gazed admiringly at her.

"What a pretty wife she would make for my son!" thought the repulsive creature.

With one bound, the toad was by the bed and he carried Thumbelina off in the nutshell. He deposited the shell in the little stream that ran through the garden so that she could not escape. Then he went to fetch his son.

The young toad, who was every bit as ugly as his father, shouted a delighted "Coac!" when he saw the sleeping child.

"Not so loud," hissed his father, "you'll wake her up. She is so light that she could get away from us. I am going to put her on that big burdock leaf in the middle of the stream. Then she'll be on an island. In the meantime, you go and prepare a comfortable room on the river bed for your wedding night."

Not long afterwards, the poor little girl woke up and discovered that she was surrounded by water and could not get back to the river's bank.

After the two toads had decorated the room with reeds, they hopped back to the burdock leaf, where Thumbelina was sobbing with fear and cold.

"May I introduce my son Hector, your husband-to-be?" said the big toad. "Your underwater home awaits you. You will be able to get married very soon!"

"Coac! Coac!" added his son, looking very stupid.

The fishes of the river had heard the old toad making his horrible plans and took pity on the little girl.

So they bit through the stalk of the leaf, tied it to a rush and towed it away downstream.

Thumbelina, very relieved at her lucky escape from the toads, happily floated along with the current until, along the way, a butterfly fluttered around her. She managed to tie her ribbon to its body and made much faster progress that way.

All at once, a big dragonfly happened to pass by, caught hold of her dress and carried her off into the air. He dropped her gently onto one of the big leaves of a tree and hovered alongside, complimenting her over and over again on her beauty and grace, and eventually introduced her to his dragonfly sisters.

"But she hasn't got any antennae!" said one.

"And she's only got two legs!" cried another.

The big dragonfly listened carefully to their objections and finally gave up the wedding plans that he had had in mind. The dragonflies abandoned Thumbelina on a daisy.

The poor thing spent the summer, and then the autumn in the forest, with only the sap of the flowers for food and the early morning dew to drink. Winter came. The big burdock leaf that had been her home shriveled up. When the snow started falling, she was so cold that she thought she would die before spring came again.

Near the forest there was a field. One day, Thumbelina found the home of an old mouse who, curiously, wore trousers and smoked a pipe.

"I've had nothing to eat for two whole days. Could you spare me a grain of corn?" she asked him.

"Come in, little one, come in and eat at once."

Later, the old mouse had a visitor, his neighbor Mr. Mole, who was as charming as could be. Mr. Mole fell in love with Thumbelina. Before very long, he asked her to marry him, but she refused his proposal.

One day, Mr. Mole invited his friends to tea. He showed them around his house, Suddenly, in one of the passageways, Thumbelina saw a swallow lying on the ground.

"Oh, pay no attention to that," was all their host said.

The little girl was very upset by this sad sight and, that night, when Mr. Mole was sound asleep, she crept back into the passageway to examine the bird. When she put her ear to its breast, she could hear a faint heartbeat. She quickly covered the swallow with a little woollen blanket to keep it warm.

When she returned to visit her patient the next night, she found the swallow awake. It told her that it had been wounded during the migration.

Every night, Thumbelina came to sit with her new friend, bringing food and comfort. When spring came, the bird was quite strong again and thinking of rejoining its companions.

Meanwhile, the old mouse had been busy with preparations for the wedding that he was determined would take place between Thumbelina and his friend Mr. Mole.

When the date of the wedding had been fixed, Thumbelina sobbed as she told her friend the swallow that she would have to live underground forever, and never see the sun.

"Would you like to come with me?" suggested the

swallow. "I am flying back to the countries where the sun shines all year round."

After a long, long journey over forests, seas and high snowcapped mountains, they finally arrived.

The swallow went back to its nest, and Thumbelina took up residence in a flower. Right next door lived a little man no higher than a thumb: the little king of the flowers.

Captivated by the beauty of his new neighbor, he very soon asked her to marry him. Thumbelina, whose heart was already his, became his wife and queen of the flowers.

At long last she had found true happiness!

The
Little Mermaid

by Hans Christian Andersen

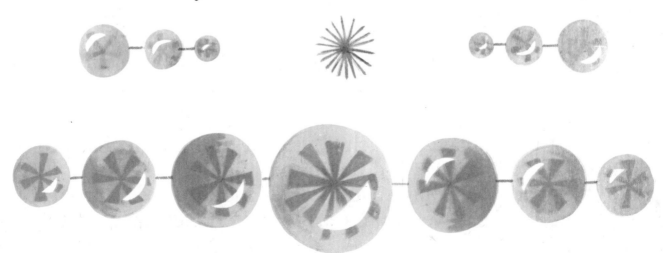

Deep under the seas, far, far deeper than any diver has ever been, is the beautiful pearl and coral domain of the king of all the seas.

His great palace of shining white marble stands on a bed of the finest white sand and, through tall crystal windows, you can see rich bunches of sea anemones and chandeliers made of roped pearls.

Here, in this watery kingdom, lives the powerful monarch who reigns over the faithful, though sometimes unruly, population of Tritons and mermaids. His subjects are half human and half fish. Like fishes, they have long supple and wavy tails. Like men, they have heads and shoulders and arms. The Tritons blow into conches in the deep sea grottos and communicate with them that way, and the mermaids have the prettiest and most captivating of voices. The songs that they sometimes sing above the surface of the waves enchant the sailors who hear them. Many sailors have even lost their lives trying to follow these enchanting singers and their haunting songs down to the bottom of the ocean.

But under the reign of good king Neptune, it was forbidden for the mermaids to ensnare unsuspecting sailors this way. However, the king, who had six daughters, did allow them, when they reached their fifteenth birthday, to swim up to the surface of the water, to play in the foam of the waves and to follow the ships from a distance as far as the coast where men lived.

The first mermaid to reach the age of fifteen came back to the underwater palace and declared,

"The sun is like a big yellow flower and it burns! It makes the foam on the waves quite warm, but I prefer the coolness

and the seaweed of my father's kingdom. It's so much more fun to slip in and out of the coral and play hide-and-seek with the starfish!"

"I swam up to the big rocky beaches," reported the second, on her return a year later. "I saw hundreds of little black and white things there, sliding and playing and diving, and bringing back fish to their babies. It must have been a colony of fishermen!"

The little princesses' grandmother who had brought them up herself, after their mother had died giving birth to the youngest, exclaimed impatiently,

"Of course not, you silly little girl. I've told you at least a hundred times about the penguins who live on the cold coasts."

And she straightened her crown of pearl oysters with a sigh. "The education of mermaid princesses really is a thankless task," she muttered. "Everything goes in one ear and out the other!"

When her turn came, the third sister surfaced amid the glistening icebergs of Greenland. She had a wonderful time playing with the polar bear cubs and the little seals in the icy waves by the shore.

The fourth sister followed the course of the great sailing ships and watched with fascination how the nimble sailors swarmed up and down the tall masts.

When the fifth returned to the underwater palace, she described the violent storm that she had witnessed with terror and amazement: the waves sweeping over onto the land, the thunder and lightning, the storm-tossed boats.

The youngest sister, poor thing, shook her long blond hair and fairly languished away with the waiting. The months seemed to stretch on and on forever and even her favorite pet fishes try as they might, could not bring a smile to light up

her pretty little face. Her grandmother scolded her,

"Your life is here with us, child, stop dreaming about land! Men are such ugly creatures, planted on two thick columns that they call legs, and on which they waddle about like ducks!"

But the little mermaid didn't believe a word of it and sighed all the more sadly as she braided chains of seaweed.

Finally, her long-awaited fifteenth birthday arrived. When the birthday feast was over, the excited little mermaid kissed her father the king and her grandmother and, followed at a distance by her sisters, she shot up to the surface like an arrow. She watched the setting sun with admiration and delight and then, as the sky darkened, she saw a magnificent ship approaching, all lit up with its sails unfurled.

As the little mermaid swam, full of wonder, toward the ship, the first flashes of lightning across the black sky warned of a terrible storm. On board, the music stopped and soon the crash of thunder was all that could be heard. The sailors were running back and forth across the dangerously sloping bridge. But in spite of their desperate efforts, the ship was engulfed by a mountainous wave.

Debris of all sorts, planks, sails and rigging, floated all around the helpless little mermaid. Then she saw the motionless body of a handsome young man floating on the waves. He had a gash in his forehead but seemed to be still breathing. The little mermaid summoned all her strength and, holding his head out of the water, she pulled him toward the beach. She hid behind a rock and called softly for help.

They waited this way for a long time and the little mermaid

worried that, without help, the poor sailor might die. Finally, a group of girls came out of a nearby church and, catching sight of the drowned man, ran down to the beach. One of them, the prettiest one, pulled a silver flask from her skirt and put it to the poor man's lips.

Seconds later, he slowly opened his eyes and looked at the girl while, in her hiding place, the little mermaid breathed a sigh of relief before diving back into the waves. But she soon realized sadly that she could not forget the handsome sailor! The seasons passed and her sadness grew deeper. Time and again she returned to the beach, full of hope, but it was in vain. After much hesitation, her grandmother, seeing her so unhappy, said,

"Child, if you can only find happiness on land, then go and

see the great witch of the deep. She alone can help you. But be very careful, the price of her services is very high indeed and the salt water of bitter tears is her favorite drink."

But the poor little mermaid was so much in love that no sacrifice seemed too great to her. She wanted to find the man who had captured her heart and no price was too high to pay. To do so, she had to assume human form and divest herself of the pretty fish tail which now seemed hideous to her because it prevented her from finding her beloved on dry land.

Braving huge eels and sharks, she dove toward the witch's lair. Swallowing her fear, she slipped through the tentacles of the giant octopus that guarded the dark grotto.

Crouching by a cauldron, a repulsive old crone was stirring a foul-smelling concoction.

"Well, well," cackled the old witch, "it looks as though the favorite daughter of the king of the seas has need of my humble services. I'm delighted to see you, my dear, delighted!

You see, I know what is tormenting you, and I know what you want, but it will cost you dearly. First, I shall take your voice because I have always wanted to sing as prettily as you. So you will be mute forever. Second, as happy as I am to give you two lovely tapering legs, every step you take will cause you great pain, but you must hide it, even when your sweet little feet start bleeding!"

"I don't care, I don't care!" cried the little mermaid. "I would gladly suffer a thousand deaths for the sake of my beloved!"

"But that's not all," the horrible crone went on, licking her lips with pleasure. "If you do not become the bride of your handsome Prince Charming, you will die without ever becoming a mermaid again."

Snatching up the cup of foul liquid that the witch handed to her, the mermaid drank it all in one gulp. As she swam away from the murky grotto, her tail became heavier and her movements awkward. Pain shot through her body. The little mermaid fainted onto the soft sand of the beach, just as her body assumed a wholly human appearance.

"Beautiful stranger, wake up!" said a voice.

When the little mermaid opened her eyes, she saw the face of her beloved leaning over her. Unfortunately, she could not answer him, but her big blue eyes were so eloquent, so full of entreaty, that the young man carried the golden-haired stranger who had lost her voice back to the nearby palace.

She captured the hearts of all who saw her, and balls and receptions were given in her honor. But the prince thought of her as a sister, as a dearly cherished friend! He confided in

her that he was hopelessly in love with an unknown stranger.

"She looks like you," he said sadly, stroking the little mermaid's hair. "I can just see her long golden hair and her blue eyes as she bent over me on the beach where I was washed up after the shipwreck. It was she who organized the rescue and alerted the palace, but then she disappeared and ever since, she has haunted my dreams. You know, sweet little sister with the lovely smile, if I had never seen her, I might even have married you."

Poor little mermaid! She suffered a thousand deaths with every step she took and all she was offered in return was the role of sister and confidante! But she still held on to one fervent hope, perhaps he would never find the object of his desire!

Alas! one fateful day, the prince visited a neighboring kingdom where he recognized one of the princesses as his golden-haired rescuer. He asked for her hand and it was granted.

The richly decorated royal flagship was to be the setting for the prince's wedding. On the bridge decorated with lights, all the nobles of the realm danced in joyous celebration. Among them, dressed in floating silks, the little mermaid leaped and spun and twirled with a broken heart.

"Just look," said the prince to his new bride, "how happy my little adopted sister is for us!"

As night fell, the poor abandoned mermaid leaned over the rails of the deck. She knew that she would soon die, because her beloved had spurned her. But she did not care, since life without love held no attraction for her.

Suddenly, voices called out from the waves beside the ship,

"You can be saved, little sister! All five of us have sold our hair to the great witch of the deep. In return, she gave us this

dagger. If you plunge it into the heart of the prince, you can come back to us. Your legs will join together to form a tail again as soon as his blood flows. Act quickly, or you'll be turned into sea spray!"

As if in a dream, the little mermaid seized the weapon and slipped into the royal bedchamber, but when she saw her love gently sleeping, she flung the dagger away from her and tiptoed away on her poor bruised little feet. Then she heard a voice say,

"Your loving heart has earned you a place among the fairies of the air. In three hundred years, you may return to the world. Sooner, perhaps, because every good deed performed by a child will mean one day less that you have to wait."

The little mermaid felt all her pain float away and she flew with the wind, a fairy of the air. But one day, as long as children remember her, she will return to the marble palace under the sea.

The Tree with the Golden Leaves

by Giambattista Basile

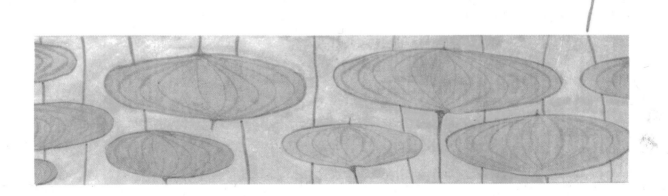

A long time ago there lived a poor farmer whose only riches were three young pigs that were tended by his three daughters.

The good man lived in a little cottage at the edge of the woods. Every day, Bertha, Mathilda, and Amanda worked in the fields, helping their father. Then, at midday, Amanda, the youngest, would go off into the woods with the three pigs. They were very partial to the acorns that lay under the dead leaves and, admiring their firm plump flesh, the farmer happily reckoned how much money they would bring the next market day. But knowing his daughter as he did, he did tend to worry and would never fail to offer a few words of advice to her, as she prepared to set off with the pigs.

"You are a good girl," he would say, "but you can be very scatterbrained and inquisitive too. Take good care of our pigs, because they are all we have in the world."

The young girl shook her golden braids and laughed, promising faithfully to be good, and vanished round the bend in the path followed by the happily grunting pigs.

One day, Amanda was sitting under an oak tree twisting a garland of ivy while her charges were snuffling around among the damp leaves. A warm September sun shone down on the clearing and, as the last swallows flew across the sky high above the treetops, the little girl fell asleep.

When she opened her eyes, Amanda was all alone. The animals had disappeared. Bursting into tears of panic and terror, she started running back and forth through the trees, calling the pigs in vain. A handsome young man suddenly stood before her startled eyes and said,

"Silly girl, why don't you look under those blankets?"

Impressed by the princely bearing of the handsome stranger, Amanda did as he suggested and found her three little pigs curled up fast asleep!

When she turned to thank the helpful stranger, he had vanished as mysteriously as he had appeared. As she got ready to return home, she noticed a young tree in the middle of a copse, its leaves shining in the light of the setting sun. Intrigued, she made her way closer to the sapling and then stopped, rooted to the spot with amazement.

The foliage of the tree was made up of leaves of pure gold. And though it looked, in every detail, like an ordinary tree, it really was made of gold! The delighted child plucked an armful of branches and ran all the way home.

With these precious leaves, wealth came into their humble home. But the farmer, who was a wise man, quickly used it to buy more land and Amanda often had to go back to the woods to remove leaves from the tree. Then one fateful morning, all she found was the bare tree trunk. So, picking up an axe, she said,

"If I cut down this useless old trunk, perhaps a strong new tree will grow and sprout more golden leaves for us."

At the first blow of the axe, the trunk disappeared and in its place, was a magnificent marble staircase.

Without a moment's hesitation, the inquisitive child ran up the steps which led her to the foot of a castle.

Built of white porcelain and crowned with golden domes,

the castle stood in the middle of a beautiful park full of flowers. Quite breathless with wonder, Amanda walked slowly on. Doors opened silently before her, but she did not see any servants. In this way, she came to the banquet hall, where a richly laid table was waiting. Amanda sat down and started hungrily eating the delicious food served there. Suddenly . . .

"No harm will come to you, little one, if you promise not to light the candles. All light is forbidden!"

These words of advice were proferred by a black-horned monster that appeared out of nowhere onto the middle of the table.

"I am not curious," she lied, quite terrified.

The monster, acting as a generous host, provided his guest with servants, a carriage and precious jewels. But Amanda's overwhelming curiosity was gnawing away at her and, one night, she set off through the palace with a lighted candle in her hand. There was no sign of her host, but in the prettiest bedroom, a handsome young man lay sleeping. She recognized him as her unknown benefactor from the woods.

"Alas, foolhardy girl, you broke your promise," cried the stranger as he woke. "With the light of your candle, you have extended the evil spell that keeps me imprisoned in the shape of a monster!"

And with a heartrending moan, the poor bewitched creature flew out of the window. Amanda burst into guilty tears and fled, only to be confronted by seven furious witches.

"Miserable child!" they howled. "Your insatiable curiosity has forced our beloved brother to keep his monstrous appearance. Poor, poor Prince Richard!"

"Have pity!" sobbed Amanda. "I didn't mean any harm. Tell me what I can do to help set the prince free."

"Very well" said the eldest of the witches. "You will have to achieve two tasks. Take this bread, this hay and this stone. Whatever you do, don't lose any one of them. If you meet a stampeding horse, throw the hay to it and it will pass you by. If a big dog chases you, throw the bread to it and it won't bite you. Finally, if a door swings open in front of the first house in the village, use this big stone to wedge it tight. Behind the door is a box of musical instruments: take it and run!

But take care. On no account are you to open that box. If you do, the wicked fairy who cast this spell will punish you cruelly. Your second and most difficult task will be to contain your insatiable curiosity."

Once again, Amanda promised faithfully, swallowed her fear in calming the stampeding horse and the ferocious dog, and seized the magical container. But, before she had gone very far, she examined the little box inquisitively.

"How on earth can musical instruments possibly fit into such a tiny thing as this? Perhaps I'll just have a little peep . . . ."

A flute, a trumpet and some bagpipes flew out, the moment she touched the lock. The instruments bounced off down the road, playing the most frenzied of tunes.

Amanda ran after them in panic.

Fear seemed to give her feet wings. She was just folding the bagpipes to put them back in the box, when Prince Richard appeared.

"My godfather, the white wizard Narcissus, finally found the spell to lift the curse that was holding me captive in the shape of a monster. Now that I am free, will you marry me, sweet Amanda?" Mischievously he added,

"I can help to cure you of your dangerous curiosity, too. It's certainly high time!"

So the story of an inquisitive little girl had a happy ending after all.

The Musicians of Bremen

of Bremen

by the Brothers Grimm

Here is the pretty story that they tell in Bremen, a lovely German town on the banks of the river Weser.

It is the members of the town's brass band who tell the story more often than anyone and you'll soon understand why . . . .

Once upon a time, in the countryside surrounding the town, there lived a man who owned a donkey.

The loyal beast had served his master faithfully for many years, carrying the vegetables that the man took to sell at the market once a week.

Alas! The donkey was growing old and weak and, one day, his master said to his wife,

"My dear, I just don't know what to do with that animal. He eats all day, he's too old to work and nobody wants to buy him . . . even for a drumskin. I haven't the heart to tie a stone around his neck and throw him in the river. So I've decided to take him into the woods and turn him loose."

"I don't think he'll be able to find his way home," said his wife in agreement.

No sooner said than done! He took the animal out into the forest and as he was a kindhearted man, he gave him a kiss before he left him there.

The little donkey didn't even try to find his way back to his stable. Not because he was as stupid as his master thought he was, but because he had heard and understood the conversation between the farmer and his wife, and he had no intention of ending up at the bottom of the river with a stone around his neck. "Where there's life, there's hope," he thought. "I could go to Bremen. I've still got a good voice (this is a delusion common to all the donkeys in the world) and I could

get a job with the town's brass band."

So, off he trotted in the direction of the town, practicing his scales all the way down the road.

Soon, he met a dog as old as he was, who was crouching against a rock and whining piteously.

"What happened to you then?" asked the donkey.

"My master decided to throw me out because I'm getting old. So I ran away from the house. When I think of all the years that I've herded his sheep and guarded his home and fetched his slippers . . . !"

"Ah, my poor friend, the ingratitude of man is past understanding. Why don't you come with me to Bremen and become a musician, too!"

Further down the road, they made the acquaintance of a cat that was sitting on the grass and meowing so that their hearts were ready to break.

In reply to the donkey's kind enquiry, the cat said,

"I've had a lucky escape! My mistress was going to drown me because, at my age, I'd rather sleep by the fire than chase mice. What's to become of me?"

"Come with us! We're going to Bremen to join the town's brass band!"

And off the three of them went.

But as they passed by a farmyard, they saw a rooster perched on the fence, crowing at the top of his voice.

"I'm singing for the last time! There are guests at the farm tomorrow and I'm going to be in the casserole for lunch!"

The donkey brayed in disbelief.

"Well, what are you waiting for then, you silly bird! Come with us to Bremen. You'll be able to use your fine voice in the brass band."

The rooster didn't wait to be asked twice. He joined them!

Meanwhile, it was getting dark and the town was still a long way off. The donkey stopped and said,

"Look over there, friends. I can see a light. Let's go and see if we can find something to eat there. If we don't eat soon, we won't have enough strength to sing."

They all agreed and headed toward the light, which they eventually saw was coming from a little house half hidden in the trees.

Peering through the window, they saw three bandits (one look at their faces and at the muskets lying beside them was enough to make that clear) who were sitting around the table eating a delicious meal.

"Mmmm, that smells so good!" murmured the dog, his nose quivering with excitement.

"We must find a way to get it!" said the donkey.

"If you put your feet up on the windowsill," the cat said to him, "then the dog can climb on your shoulders, I can climb onto his head and the rooster can sit on mine. Then we'll go in singing as loud as we can!"

They broke the window and launched into a chorus that was as extraordinary as it was terrifying!

On hearing such a din and on seeing such an incredible apparition, the bandits thought they were being attacked by a swarm of demons. They ran off into the forest, as fast as their legs would carry them.

The four animals laughed and laughed and rushed to devour the excellent meal. Then, they put out the light, settled down comfortably and fell asleep. All, that is, except for the cat, who was the shrewdest of them all!

Was there something on his mind?

At midnight, the bandits sent one of their men back to the house, to see if the demons had gone.

The unlucky scout set off on his chief's orders, but his legs were shaking with fear. As he stepped into the cottage, he caught sight of the cat's eyes glowing in the dark. He had never seen anything like it and he was terrified!

He tried to escape but a loud "cockadoodledoo" woke the donkey who lashed out a tremendous kick to the intruder's backside.

In panic, the poor bandit dashed for the door where the

dog was waiting for him. The dog started barking and biting him as hard as he could and sent him screaming on his way.

When he finally rejoined his companions, the bandit's hair had turned pure white with shock.

Stammering and stuttering, he eventually managed to describe what he had seen and heard in the house.

The bandits abandoned their lair and left the area for good, leaving behind all the ill-gotten riches they had acquired over the many long years that they had terrorized the region.

Back at the little house, the four animals celebrated their victory all night long with a deafening chorus of crowing and braying and barking and meowing. Finally, quite exhausted, they fell asleep in a corner, and all was quiet once more.

The night's infernal commotion had been heard all over the neighborhood and a few intrepid souls ventured into the forest to try and find out what had caused it, because nobody could remember ever hearing such a din in those parts.

They brought back the astonishing news to the town. It spread like wildfire and soon everyone had heard it.

Then the people of Bremen realized that, at last, they were free of the bandits forever and, with the brass band marching at their head, they set off to thank their brave liberators. They were so grateful that they promised to see that the animals would never want for anything and to always treat them with respect and affection. Finally the little band had found real friends who would protect them always.

Tom Thumb

by the Brothers Grimm

A poor peasant was unhappy that he and his wife had no children.

"Oh dear!" sighed his wife. "If we could only have just one and even if he were no bigger than your thumb, I would be so happy!"

And nine months later, they had a son who was so small that they named him Tom Thumb.

His father made him a tiny bed out of a nutshell and both of his parents loved their little boy very much.

Time passed, but Tom Thumb didn't get any bigger. His parents did not worry about this at all. He was just exactly what they had wished for.

Although Tom Thumb was small, he was a child of rare intelligence and courage.

One day, he absolutely insisted on accompanying his father who was going to the woods to collect logs for the winter. In view of his size, all he could collect were twigs.

Two strangers happened to pass by and were astonished at how small and how cute Tom was. Then it occurred to them that they could earn a lot of money by exhibiting him at the village fair. They approached the peasant.

"Sell us your little man, we promise to look after him very well!" they proposed.

"No!" said the father flatly. "He's my son and I wouldn't part with him for all the gold in the world!"

And he wouldn't hear another word about it, but Tom Thumb climbed up onto his father's shoulder and whispered in his ear,

"Sell me, father, sell me. I'll be back before you even know I'm gone!"

So the father agreed to give up his son for a shining gold piece, and the two strangers walked away delighted with their extraordinary purchase.

By the time night fell, they had walked a long, long way.

In the dark, Tom Thumb waited until his new masters were looking the other way and made his escape. He climbed up into the branches of a nearby tree and hid in an abandoned bird's nest.

Furious at having been tricked by the little man, the two strangers searched high and low for him. But in vain! Finally, they went grumbling on their way without him.

Snug in his hiding place, Tom Thumb fell fast asleep. In

the middle of the night, he was awakened by the sound of voices. Two thieves had stopped at the foot of the tree to discuss their wicked plans.

"How can we get our hands on the king's treasure?" one of them asked the other.

"That's easy," Tom Thumb piped up, "I'll explain it to you."

And nimbly, without making a sound, he slipped down from his perch high in the tree while the astonished thieves looked around everywhere to find the mysterious speaker. Tom Thumb explained his plan and the two men decided to take this unexpected partner-in-crime along with them.

They set off in the direction of the royal palace and managed to slip past the sleeping guards into the palace

grounds. They went straight to the treasure chamber and pushed Tom Thumb in through the bars on the window.

"We'll wait for you out here. Find as many jewels as you can and pass them out to us."

"Tell me where to look for them then," cried Tom Thumb at the top of his voice.

"Shush! Keep your voice down!" hissed his companions, glancing around them in alarm.

Pretending that he hadn't heard them, Tom Thumb started shouting as loud as he could:

"Hurray! I've found a big chest full of treasure!"

"Be quiet, you little wretch!" growled the thieves. "You'll wake the whole palace and get us caught!"

Tom Thumb yelled all the louder.

"Do you want necklaces, bracelets or rings? Oh, and there are some crowns, too! Do you want everything? Tell me quickly so that I know what to take."

In vain his companions ordered him to keep quiet.

It was already too late! Lights were going on in all the windows of the palace. Armed to the teeth, guards were pouring out of every door shouting,

"Stop, thief! Stop, thief!"

But the thieves weren't waiting to be caught. They had run off as fast as their legs would carry them and were already far away across the fields.

In the treasure chamber, the soldiers found Tom Thumb who told them how it was his idea to raise the alarm, so that the thieves' wicked plans would be foiled.

There had been so much commotion that the king, who was eating his supper, interrupted his meal and asked for an explanation of the disturbances. He ordered that the person who had so bravely safeguarded his treasures be brought to him at once.

Overcome with shyness, Tom Thumb walked across the table to where the king was sitting.

"So," said the king, "it is thanks to you that I still have my jewels. I would like to reward you for your quick thinking. My Treasurer will give you a hundred pieces of gold immediately!"

Delighted at his unexpected fortune, Tom Thumb set off on his way home but, quite exhausted by all his adventures, he lay down on the fragrant grass of a meadow and fell fast asleep, under a tree.

When he woke up, Tom Thumb found himself in the stomach of a lamb which had swallowed him along with a mouthful of grass. He was trying to work out a way of escaping from this prison when the lamb was eaten by a wolf.

Tom Thumb called out to the wolf as loudly as he could with his little voice,

"Dear Mr. Wolf, would you like a really good meal?"

"Who's that?" said the startled wolf.

Then, unable to contain his greed, he listened to what the voice had to say.

Tom Thumb told him the shortest way to his parents' house.

The ferocious beast followed the instructions of the mysterious voice from his insides and slipped into the kitchen where he started devouring everything in sight.

Tom Thumb was starting to feel rather cramped in the stomach of the lamb that was in the even more crowded stomach of the wolf. So he called his parents at the top of his voice. They came running at once to free him.

With a single blow of his axe, the father killed the wolf and, to his joy, released the lamb and his son.

With the gold pieces given to him by the king, Tom Thumb and his parents lived happily ever after.

The Beautiful Dove

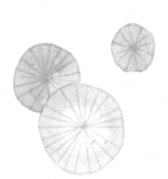

by Giambattista Basile

Once upon a time there was a little old woman who lived in a tumble-down cottage on the edge of a large forest of fig trees and poplars.

This old woman, who was called Myrtle, was very poor, so poor that she had to spend all day begging for just enough food to keep body and soul together.

One day, while she was out walking, she was lucky enough to meet a kind person who gave her a big basket brimming with peas and beans.

Myrtle went home very happy, her mouth was watering just thinking about the delicious meal she was going to cook.

No sooner was she home, than she put the peas and the beans into her best earthenware pot, placed the pot on the windowsill and set off into the woods to collect some logs for her fire.

Soon afterwards, Maxime, the son of the king, happened to pass that way, as he was out hunting. When he saw the pot on the windowsill, he said to his attendant knights,

"I'll wager you that I can smash that pot to pieces with a single shot!"

Taking long and careful aim, he shattered it to smithereens, and its precious contents were scattered in the mud.

At that moment, the poor old woman returned. When she saw her long-awaited meal lying trampled on the ground, she turned and cursed the prince.

"You scoundrel!" she cried. "You didn't spare a thought for my misery, did you? Well, you will be punished for this. You will fall in love with the daughter of a wicked ogress and you will have to suffer many ordeals."

When he heard these words, the prince just burst out

laughing and rode off without even bothering to reply.

A little later the prince lost sight of his companions and met a beautiful young girl who was picking flowers to fill the basket on her arm.

Maxime spoke to her and the young girl, whose name was Sunflower, replied in the sweetest of tones.

"You are so beautiful and so sweet that I think I am already in love with you!" said the prince.

The words had hardly left his lips when an ogress, of quite terrifying ugliness, sprang out from behind a bush. She glared at the prince and cackled evilly,

"How dare you court my daughter with such compliments!" she barked. "I don't know who you might be, but you're certainly going to find out who I am!"

She seized the young man by the scruff of the neck, as if he were no more than a common and troublesome rabbit, and pushed him into an enormous field.

"If you don't want me to eat you alive," she threatened, rolling her eyes and spitting with fury, "you'll have this whole field dug and sown by tonight!"

The prince paled. He would never be able to finish the work in one day . . . . Not even if he were a giant!

But as soon as the ogress had gone, Sunflower came up to the unfortunate prince and tried to console him.

"Don't despair! I will help you, if you like!"

And thanks to the magic powers at her command, the field was dug and sown within minutes, without the prince having to move so much as a finger.

At dusk, the ogress returned. When she realized that the task she had set him had been completed to perfection, her eyes blazed with rage, as she decreed,

"Since you are so wonderfully efficient, by tomorrow you can split every single log in that huge pile over there. Get to work at once!"

Once again, gentle Sunflower used her magic powers to help the prince.

Unfortunately, the ogress had an extremely suspicious nature. She guessed that her daughter had helped Maxime and said to him,

"I will give you twenty-four hours to empty that cistern. It holds a million gallons of water. And, above all, you must do it alone. If anyone helps you, it will be the end of you!"

The young girl wisely and earnestly advised the prince to take flight.

"My mother knows that I helped you to accomplish the tasks that she set you to do. If you succeed in emptying the cistern as well, her revenge will be terrible!"

As if by magic, Sunflower conjured up a long underground tunnel which led to the nearby town and, from there, the young girl and her companion fled towards the palace of the king. On the way, they stopped at a little country inn.

"Wait for me here!" said the prince. "I shall go to the palace and get a carriage, servants and clothes because I love you and I want to marry you!"

Meanwhile, the ogress had returned home and had discovered, to her extreme annoyance, that both her daughter and the young man had disappeared.

She was furious.

"May the prince no longer have any memory of Sunflower!" she screeched, tearing her hair out with rage. "May he forget her completely at the precise instant that he arrives at the palace and receives the first kiss!"

Now, it so happened that the prince's mother ran to greet her son on the great marble staircase and that she kissed him

with tears of relief and joy. In that instant, all memory of Sunflower was wiped from his mind.

His mother announced,

"The Princess of Flanders has come to visit us! She is very rich and elegant and also exceptionally pretty. I think you will make a very handsome couple! The wedding will take place in a week!"

The young man agreed willingly and gave the order to begin the preparations for the marriage. There was not much time and the whole palace, from the cellars to the attics, bustled with frantic activity.

Meanwhile, Sunflower was impatiently waiting at the inn for Maxime's return.

She was heartbroken when she heard from the innkeeper

that the prince was about to be married to a beautiful young princess.

But, despite the cruel pain she was suffering, she did not hesitate for a moment. She disguised herself as a man and went to the palace to find out for herself if what she had been told was true.

She asked for directions to the royal kitchen and applied to work as a kitchen hand. As there was a great deal of work to be done, she was hired on the spot.

A few days before Maxime's wedding to the Princess of Flanders, the prince was served a magnificent cake decorated with marzipan and fruits. He cut into it. As he did, a white dove flew out of the cake and sang sweetly,

"Have you forgotten the one who saved your life and who loves you so dearly?"

The prince looked very troubled for a moment, then he ordered:

"Send for the person who baked this cake!"

It was Sunflower who had baked the cake. As soon as Maxime saw her again, he recognized her at once and remembered all her kindness and sweetness and the promise he had made to her when they parted. Then they went for a long walk together, they had so much to tell each other.

Soon afterwards, Maxime and Sunflower were married amid the most joyous celebrations throughout the kingdom. The poor Princess of Flanders, not a little cross, had to make her way home alone.

Little Brother and Little Sister

and

Little Sister

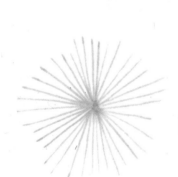

by the Brothers Grimm

Little Brother and Little Sister had had the misfortune of losing their mother. They had felt very much alone since her death, so they were very pleased when their father decided to marry again. They were hoping that some happiness would come back to their lives.

But, alas! Their stepmother, a cruel and wicked witch, hated them and found any excuse to punish them harshly.

One day, Little Brother took his sister's hand and said,

"We haven't had a single day's peace ever since our father remarried. Our stepmother beats us and gives us only stale crusts of bread to eat. She treats the dog better than she treats us! Let's leave, and try to find somewhere where we can live without being ill-treated. We'll find it, even if we have to search the whole world over!"

"You are right, Little Brother, we have to go, we will never be happy here!"

So the next day, while their stepmother was fast asleep after a heavy breakfast, Little Brother and Little Sister crept out of the house and ran away into the woods.

All day long, they trudged hand in hand across fields and meadows, through woods and across streams, until they were far, far away from home.

Toward evening, they found themselves in a big forest. They were so tired after their long walk, so miserable and so very hungry, that they hid inside an old hollow tree trunk, curled up together and fell asleep in no time.

Next morning when the two children woke up, the sun was already high in the sky. It was a beautiful day and getting hotter and hotter by the minute.

"I'm so thirsty, Little Sister!" cried the boy, as they climbed out of the tree trunk. "Let's go and look for a river or a spring where we can drink."

But, the witch had seen her husband's children leave and she had followed them, unnoticed, hiding behind the trees in the forest and casting spells over every spring and every river that she passed. She knew very well that, sooner or later, the two children would need a drink.

When the runaways arrived beside a pretty sparkling stream, Little Brother ran to the bank. Suddenly, Little

Sister heard a rustling murmur. "Whoever drinks of my water will be turned into a deer!"

"Don't drink it, Little Brother, you'll be turned into a deer!" she cried frantically. "Don't drink it! The water's bewitched!"

But it was too late, Little Brother was kneeling over the stream, drinking in great gulps. When he raised his head, Little Sister saw that he had turned into a little spotted deer.

"My poor brother!" she cried. "What is to become of us? What can we do?"

The deer leaped into her arms. Big, shiny tears were running down his muzzle.

The little girl hugged him tight, dried his tears and tenderly consoled him.

"No matter what may happen, we shall never be parted, my dear Little Brother!" she said. "Come along, let's go now."

They walked on together until, many hours later, they came across a little house nestling in a clearing. "It looks abandoned," Little Sister said. "This might be a good place for us to settle down."

With the deer at her heels, Little Sister inspected the house. It could have been made just for them. She went to gather some dry leaves to make a bed for her brother. Then she picked some wild berries and sweet grass for him to eat.

Years went by and the children grew up in peace and happiness.

Little Sister never got bored because the deer, who had

retained his power of speech, could converse with her and accompany her on long walks.

One day, the young king of the country organized a royal hunting party. The sound of horns and the barking of the hounds echoed through the forest. The deer was pawing the ground with excitement and impatience inside the little house, begging his sister to let him out. Finally she agreed, telling him to be back before nightfall and to knock on the door with the password "Little Sister, let me in!"

The little deer happily promised to do so and ran out into the clearing. The hunt was on its way. The king caught sight of him and gave chase.

The deer was having the time of his life, leaping out under

the noses of his pursuers time after time and then vanishing again just before they could catch him.

Night was falling as he knocked on the door of the little house and gave the password. Then, exhausted by his frolics, he fell into his sister's arms.

But the king had followed the animal to his home and, intrigued by what he had seen and heard, knocked at the door saying "Little Sister, let me in!" When Little Sister opened the door, he was very surprised to come face to face with such a beautiful girl in such an unexpected place.

"I am sorry that I chased your deer," he said, "and I am delighted that he seems to have come to no harm."

Then Little Sister told him the sad story of their lives. The

king offered to take them both back with him to live at the palace and swore to force their wicked stepmother to break her spell on Little Brother.

The young king soon fell in love with Little Sister and, some time later, they were married. He sent messengers to see the witch, to ask her to release Little Brother from the spell that kept him imprisoned in animal form.

When she found out that her stepchildren were still alive, the witch flew into a terrible rage, refused to lift the spell and, what is more, swore to take her revenge! She had already murdered her husband, their father.

A year went by. The queen had a beautiful baby son.

When the witch heard news of the baby's birth, she was overcome with jealousy. She waited until the king had gone hunting with the prince of a neighboring land, kidnapped his wife and threw her into prison.

Every day, she stood at the window of her cell and taunted her. She told her that her husband was dead, killed by a wild boar, and that she would never see her son again. The poor queen cried all the time.

But finally the king returned and when he heard what had happened, he put his mother-in-law on trial for witchcraft. Upon her death, a few days later, the deer fell to the ground. To the utter amazement of the courtiers, a young man shrugged off the animal's skin and stood up. It was Little Brother!

Little Brother and the king set off immediately to search for the queen. They found her crouched in the deepest dungeon of the castle owned by the witch.

Reunited at last, Little Brother clasped his sister in his arms and swore to stay at her side forever.

Then the queen, crying with happiness, kissed her son whom everyone agreed was certainly the most beautiful baby in the world.

So the young king and queen lived happily ever after, surrounded by their loyal subjects. As for Little Brother, shortly afterwards, he married the king's prettiest sister.

The Goose Girl

by the Brothers Grimm

Once upon a time, there was a wise king who reigned over a prosperous land.

He lived in a magnificent castle with his beautiful queen and their three daughters.

Martha, his eldest daughter had hair as black as ebony; the locks of her sister Cornelia were the color of flames, while Floralinda, the youngest, was golden blonde. Her eyes were blue and sparkled like diamonds. She was the prettiest of the three sisters.

She had received a precious gift from her fairy godmother. When she cried, her tears turned into pearls.

The king, who was called Seraphim, loved his three daughters equally. But as he grew older, he began to worry. Which one of them should he appoint to succeed him to the throne?

"Children," he said, "one of you must follow me as ruler of this country, but I do not know which one to choose. So I have decided to put you to a test. The one who can prove that she loves me the best will rule in my place."

Martha and Cornelia found pretty words of flattery to convince their father that they loved him more than anything in the world.

Floralinda, who was much shyer, said simply,

"Daddy, I love you very much. I love you as much as salt because, without salt, nothing has any taste."

This comparison struck the old king as highly disrespectful.

"How dare you speak to your father like that!" he cried angrily. "Well, you will be punished for this! Leave the

country at once, and I forbid you to set foot in this castle again!"

Desperately humiliated, poor Floralinda said tearful farewells to her sisters and left the court.

For many weeks, she walked all day, with no food but the berries she found in the forest and no bed but the soft moss under the trees.

Meanwhile, King Seraphim regretted having exiled his daughter and gave orders for his most trusted courtiers to set off in search of her to bring her back to the palace. His envoys scoured the country but all their efforts were in vain. Nobody had seen or heard of the princess.

Three years went by. For the king and queen, they were years of anguish and sorrow. They had no idea what had become of Floralinda and gave up hope of ever seeing her again.

One morning, Prince Benedict arrived at the palace gate.
He had left the land of the Magic Springs, over which he
reigned, on a lengthy journey. His stay at the court of King
Seraphim was very pleasant indeed and, when the time came
for his departure, he asked for an audience with the queen.

"Madam!" he said. "In return for the kind hospitality you
have shown me, please accept the gift of these two pearls."

The queen caught her breath when she saw that the two
pearls of which he spoke were none other than two of her
beloved Floralinda's tears!

"My prince, I beg of you, tell me who gave you these
pearls!" she cried and her heart was filled with hope.

"They were given to me, a few months ago, by a kind old
woman. She lives in the forest of the Blue Lake together with
a beautiful young lady who looks after the geese."

"Seraphim! Seraphim!" called the queen, as soon as the young man had finished speaking.

"What's happening?" asked the king.

"Oh Seraphim, didn't you hear? Our Floralinda is alive. She is living in the forest of the Blue Lake and she's become a goose girl!" said the poor mother bursting into tears.

Without further ado, the king and queen set off in search of the mysterious old woman. They were accompanied by their courtiers and Prince Benedict who led the way.

They traveled for many days and nights and finally came to a halt in front of a tumbledown little hovel.

As soon as they knocked on the door, the old woman opened it and said quite naturally,

"Pray enter my modest abode! I've been waiting for you."
Then, turning to the king, she continued,

"Three years ago, King Seraphim, if you had been able to control your temper, you would have spared your poor wife and yourself much sorrow . . . and you would not have caused your daughter Floralinda to suffer as she has. Because for three years, she has lived the hard life of a goose girl. And she has done so dressed in rags and subjected to poverty and want. Yet nobody has ever heard a word of complaint pass her lips and if a cloud ever passed across her smiling face, it was because she was haunted by the memory of your anger and your rejection of her love. Now, it is high time that she knew a little real happiness in her life again!"

And before the king had time to utter a word, the old woman called out,

"Floralinda! Floralinda!"

In answer to the call, a door opened and a young woman stood there with long hair the color of gold and eyes that sparkled like two diamonds. She was beautiful!

With tears of joy, the young princess threw herself into her parents' arms and kissed them.

The young king of the land of the Magic Springs had stood to one side to watch the happy reunion.

He gazed in speechless admiration at the beauty and grace of the princess.

Just then, the old woman intervened.

"Dearest Floralinda! As a reward for your patience during your three long years of uncomplaining misery, I bequeath this cottage to you, and all the treasures hidden in it!"

She kissed her young friend tenderly and disappeared as if by magic, and nobody ever heard tell of her again.

Then suddenly, a miracle! A deafening clap of thunder rocked the little hovel to its foundations and it was transformed into a magnificent palace with a roof of pure gold and high white walls of ivory.

With her parents and Prince Benedict, Floralinda returned to her home where everyone was waiting to give her a rousing welcome, especially her sisters who loved her dearly.

Soon afterwards, she married the prince who was, in a way, responsible for her rediscovered happiness. The whole country joined in the wedding festivities which lasted a whole week!

And so the little goose girl began a new life as a happy and beloved bride.

Her father deeply regretted his mistaken judgement of her.

But Floralinda proved her love for him once more by forgiving him for his unjust anger.

She sometimes thought about her years of hardship and always said a little prayer of thanks to heaven for having guided Prince Benedict to the door of the old woman's hovel.

She would have liked to thank her benefactress too, for her help and for her gifts, but she had completely disappeared.

When Floralinda had children of her own, their favorite bedtime story was the one about the little goose girl, but they never found out that their mother was its heroine!

The Fairies

by Charles Perrault

Once upon a time, in a little village at the edge of a large wood, a widow lived with her two daughters.

The elder, whose name was Bertha, was so like her mother in character and appearance, that one could hardly tell them apart.

Both of them were so unpleasant that nobody in the village had ever had any desire to even speak to them, let alone seek out their company or make friends with them.

By contrast, Mathilda, the younger, had all her dear father's gentle goodness, and there was not a young girl for miles around who could compare with her in beauty.

There is a proverb that says that birds of a feather flock together, or, in other words, that people who are like each other, like each other.

The widow loved her elder daughter very much and for the younger, she had nothing but hatred and contempt.

Poor Mathilda was forced to eat alone in the kitchen and to work from morning till night.

She had to wash all the dishes, make all the beds and sweep the stairs every day.

As if that were not bad enough, she had to sleep on an old straw mattress in a tiny storeroom, while Bertha's room was the largest and most richly decorated in the house, lined with mirrors in which she never tired of admiring herself.

What is more, twice a day, Mathilda went to fetch water from a spring in the middle of the wood and struggled back home bent over from the weight of the heavy pitcher.

The poor girl submitted to all this work and all the indignities heaped upon her without complaint. But at night, when she was alone in her little room, she could not help

crying when she remembered her dear dead father whom she had loved so much.

One day, while she was drawing water at the spring, a little old lady came up to her and, in a hoarse and quavering voice, asked her for a drink of water from her pitcher.

"Why, of course, dear lady!" said Mathilda.

She rinsed out her pitcher, drew fresh water from the spring and helped the old lady quench her thirst.

"Thank you," she said, wiping her lips. "You are so kind and so pretty that I would like to give you a gift. Every time you open your mouth to speak, either a flower or a precious stone will fall from your lips."

The old lady was in fact a fairy who had disguised herself as a poor peasant woman to test the young girl's charity and kindness.

When Mathilda returned home, her mother scolded her for having wasted so much time.

"So, you think you can go off for walks, with all the work you have to do here . . . . I'll teach you!"

"Oh Mother, please forgive me for having been so long!" said Mathilda, and two roses and two pearls fell out of her mouth.

"What – what's happened to you, girl?" asked her mother in amazement.

Mathilda told her of her strange meeting with the old lady at the spring.

"Here's a chance for us to make our fortune!" her mother cried. "But it isn't fair that you alone should have this precious gift. I'm going to send your sister to the spring.

Come here, Bertha, look what came out of your sister's mouth when she spoke. Wouldn't you like the same thing to happen to you? It's easy! All you have to do is go to the spring and when a poor old woman asks you for a drink, give it to her."

"You don't seriously expect me to go and fetch water! Well, I just won't" cried Bertha in outrage.

But eventually, her mother managed to convince her, and she set off to fetch water in a magnificent silver jug.

Almost as soon as she reached the spring, a young woman appeared wearing beautiful clothes and magnificent jewels.

"Could you spare me a drink of water?" she asked politely.

"Who do you take me for . . . your servant?" Bertha

exclaimed. "If you're thirsty, drink from the spring!"

The woman was the same fairy who had appeared to Mathilda, but this time she had disguised herself as a princess.

"How very uncharitable you are," said the fairy, very calmly and without a trace of anger. "You shall receive the gift that you deserve too. With every word you utter, a toad or a snake will come out of your mouth."

Bertha shrugged her shoulders impatiently and went back home.

"Well? What gift did you get from the old woman?" her mother asked her immediately. "Tell me quickly!"

"Mother," the young girl started to say and stopped immediately as dozens of toads sprang out of her mouth.

"Oh no!" her mother shrieked, jumping back with horror. "What's gone wrong? This must be your sister's doing, and she'll pay dearly for it too!"

To escape from her mother's unjust rage, Mathilda fled into the woods and spent the night hiding behind a tree crying bitterly.

The next morning, the king's son, on his way back to the palace from a hunting trip, saw her sitting there and stopped.

"What are you doing here, all alone in the woods?" he asked her with kind concern.

"Oh sir! How good of you to concern yourself with my sad story."

And she wept as she told him her story and the events that had brought her to be alone in the woods that day. Naturally, while she spoke, precious stones and flowers flowed from her lips until they covered the ground all around her. The prince was so moved by her story and enchanted by her magical powers that he took her back to the royal palace where he introduced her to his father and to all the court dignitaries.

Her sweet and gentle nature soon won all their hearts.

A few days later, the royal heralds announced throughout the kingdom that the prince and Mathilda were to be married.

The streets of the capital were brimming with happy

crowds. The farmers put on their best Sunday clothes and came to bring their gifts to the young couple, including the finest fruit from their orchards, the finest wine from their vineyards, the finest and wooliest sheep from their flocks. But, above all, they brought their love and loyalty to the newlyweds.

The wedding ceremony was celebrated amid great pomp and rejoicing, and Mathilda and her prince lived happily ever after.

But what became of Bertha?

At first she was delighted to be rid of her younger sister. Then she flew into such a terrible jealous rage when she heard of Mathilda's marriage to the prince that she left the village the next day and nobody ever saw or heard of her again.

The Underground Prison

by the Brothers Grimm

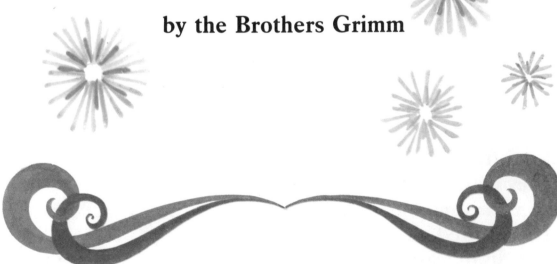

A long long time ago, there was a king who had three very beautiful daughters. He was very rich and owned a splendid castle that stood in a vast park.

In the park there were all sorts of different fruit trees that the king was very fond of. But the one he preferred to all the others was an apple tree that, according to legend, came from Paradise and which, therefore, produced the finest, most marvelous apples in the whole wide world. The tree had been a present to the king from his fairy godmother. It had been decreed that if any person dared to pick a single apple from the tree, they would find themselves locked up at once in an underground prison.

Every day, the king's daughters walked in the park and stopped in front of the apple tree. They sighed as they looked longingly at the shiny, red, mouth-watering apples.

"What a shame that we can't pick just one of them! Perhaps the wind will shake some of them down?"

But days passed and not a single apple fell to the ground. Then the youngest daughter said to her sisters,

"Do you know what I think? I think that the decree only applies to strangers and not to us. Our father loves us too much to punish us just for picking an apple!"

"That's true!" said her sisters. "Since the tree belongs to our father, it belongs to us as well. So we must be allowed to pick its fruit!"

They couldn't resist the temptation any longer and each of them picked an apple. In that instant, the earth opened up and swallowed all three of them.

The disappearance of his daughters plunged the king into

the depths of despair. He proclaimed an edict throughout the land that he would give one of them in marriage to the man who brought them all home safe and well.

A great many young men set off immediately in search of the three princesses, for they were so pretty and so sweet that they were beloved of all their subjects. The searchers scoured the country from end to end, but in vain. The king's daughters were nowhere to be found.

Among their number were three young huntsmen who had also set out in search of the princesses. After they had walked for days and days, they came to a large forest.

They decided to search it. Every day, they all went off in

different directions, and every evening they would meet up again in the same place. None of them had found any trace of the princesses and they were beginning to feel discouraged.

Then, one day, Martin, the youngest of the huntsmen, met a dwarf along the way.

"I'm very hungry!" the dwarf said, "Could you give me something to eat?"

"Here," said Martin who was very kindhearted, "take my lunch: a piece of bread and an apple."

The dwarf quickly devoured the food Martin gave him.

"Now it is my turn to help you," he declared. "I know you are looking for the king's daughters, and I know where you can find them. Come with me and I'll show you."

The dwarf led Martin right into the heart of the forest and there he pointed out the opening of a very deep well.

"The princesses are at the bottom of that well, you have my word on it," he said.

Martin thanked the dwarf and ran to fetch his two companions. He told them what had happened and showed them the well. They decided that one of them would climb into a basket and the other two would lower it to the bottom with a rope. Since Martin was the lightest, he was the one who went down the well.

When he got to the bottom, he saw the three princesses who entreated him in tears,

"Oh, brave huntsman! Help us please! We want to get out of here!"

Suddenly, Martin saw a dragon in the corner of the well. It was growling with menace and spitting out great tongues of flame. He approached and bravely attacked it. The furious dragon reared up on its hind legs. As it towered above him, Martin quickly plunged his sword into its belly.

Then he helped the princesses climb into the basket and, one by one, his companions pulled them up to the surface. But when it came to his turn, he waited in vain for the basket to descend again. The other two had gone off and abandoned him at the bottom of the well!

Helpless, Martin sat sadly on the floor of the well and then he saw a little flute lying beside him. He picked it up, hoping that someone might hear it. He started to play. The little dwarf he had met before appeared at once and with him, a whole host of other dwarves.

"What would you like?" he asked Martin. "Your wish is our command."

"I want to be outside this well," said Martin, "and see the light of the sun again!"

The dwarves picked him up and, some pulling, others pushing, they hoisted him right up to the top of the well. As soon as his feet touched the ground, Martin went straight to the king's castle, where he arrived just as they were about to celebrate the weddings of the two eldest princesses.

He ran up the stairs to the great hall of the castle where he found the king with his three daughters and the two other huntsmen. When she saw him, the youngest girl cried out,

"Father! That's him, he's the one who saved us! He killed the dragon and the others just abandoned him at the bottom of the well!"

When he heard this, the king flew into a black rage.

"What!" he thundered, as the two huntsmen cowered in terror. "Miserable wretches! You were dishonest and cowardly enough to condemn your companion to languish at the bottom of the well, were you? Well, now it's your turn to go to prison! Guards, take them to the dungeons!"

The two huntsmen hung their heads with shame as they were led away.

"I thank you most gratefully for saving the lives of my daughters," the king addressed Martin. "I give you the hand of one of them in marriage, as I promised I would. Which do you choose?"

Martin, who had fallen in love with the youngest of the

princesses, looked at her and the young girl smiled at him.

"Hmm! I see that you've already made up your mind!" said the king, laughing. Then he asked the princess,

"What do you say, my daughter? Do you agree?"

"Oh yes, father!" the princess replied flushed with emotion. "He is so good and so brave!"

So Martin the huntsman was married to the youngest of the three princesses, who was also the prettiest and the sweetest. And from that day on, he was as happy as a king!

The Garden of Paradise

by Hans Christian Andersen

Once, a young prince reigned over a wide and wealthy land.

His subjects loved him so dearly that they would have given their lives to satisfy the merest of his whims.

Yet the young man always seemed so sad. There was never even a shadow of a smile to light his face.

His grandmother was the only person who could entertain him by telling him fantastic stories that he loved to listen to. One of them had particularly captured his imagination. It was called "The Garden of Paradise."

"Tell it again, grandmother," the young man would beg, when the old lady had finished the tale.

So his grandmother would patiently begin the story once more:

"The garden is a wonderful place, created centuries ago, where Adam and Eve lived. Every one of its trees bears fruits that are as enormous as they are delicious. They have infinite properties. Every flower is a delicious sweetmeat that can impart all the education one may desire.

For example, the rose is made of sugar candy and imparts a gift for mathematics. The lily, made of marzipan, gives knowledge of literature. The gardenia, which flowers in abundance, gives a bronze colored liquid which transmits musical genius."

"Oh! I would love to visit the Garden of Paradise, grandmother!" sighed the prince. "But how will I ever be able to find my way there?"

Gradually, the idea took such a firm hold on his mind that he fell into a deep depression.

All the doctors of the kingdom were consulted, as well as

the most powerful magicians. They all agreed in their diagnosis: the prince would never be happy again unless he visited the fabled garden.

But not one of them could produce any suggestion at all as to where it might be found.

Meanwhile, the prince's despair worsened. One day, he went to see the queenmother and declared,

"Mother, I simply can't bear to mope around like this any longer. It's so cold and so sad here. I've decided to go and look for the Garden of Paradise that Grandmother has told me so much about. I shall not return until I have found it.

In my absence, I leave the kingdom in your care."

The queen was very upset, because the prince had never left her before, and tried to dissuade him, telling him that his grandmother had a very vivid imagination and that the

miraculous garden probably didn't even exist. But nothing could sway the young man's determination.

Finally, the queen ran out of arguments, kissed her son tenderly and begged him to take good care of himself on his travels, wherever they might take him.

As soon as he had taken leave of his mother, the prince went to the stables and had his best charger saddled. Then he galloped out of the castle gates.

He rode for miles along bumpy paths, then through dense undergrowth that scratched his face as he pushed through it.

After a week, he came to the edge of a deep forest. His horse shied rather than plunge into the dense dark woods, but the prince spurred it on.

Suddenly, with a roar of thunder, a violent storm broke. The trees were bent almost to the ground by the raging wind and the very earth seemed to tremble, as all the little animals of the forest ran to take whatever cover they could find.

In spite of the thunder and the blinding flashes of lightning, the prince managed to find a grotto for shelter.

To his great surprise, he found that the refuge was already occupied: an old woman was standing in front of a roaring wood fire.

The prince, drenched from head to foot and shivering with cold, stopped at the entrance, but the woman invited him in.

"Come in by the fire and dry your clothes, you'll catch a cold. I am the mother of the four winds," she informed him.

"Who are the four winds, old woman?" he asked.

"Why, my sons, of course! And unruly lads they are too, believe me, they keep me very busy when they're not off roaming the world! Ah, here comes North Wind now! I can tell it's him by the gust of cold air. You must meet him!"

And just then, a big creature covered with frost came in.

"Hello mother! I'm back from the Icy Sea. My word, it's hot in here! I'm stif–"

Before he could finish his sentence, West Wind burst into the grotto. He was rather scantily dressed.

"I simply can't find my stupid brother! Hey, it's rather cold in here, isn't it!"

While the two winds were engaged in their usual squabble about the temperature of the grotto, South Wind made his entrance, wearing nothing but a loincloth.

"Now you listen to me, brothers. I tell you it's so cold in here that you could freeze a whole lion in a matter of minutes. Give me the Sahara desert any day!" he said laughing.

The young man, rather frightened by the sight of these three winds arguing in voices as loud as thunder claps, had shrunk into a dark corner. Suddenly, East Wind, dressed as a mandarin, slipped soundlessly into their midst.

He was a pleasant-faced and distinguished little man. He kissed the old woman and said,

"I've come straight from Japan, mother. Life there is very peaceful and very agreeable but I'm glad to be home."

"Will you be going to the Garden of Paradise soon?" his mother enquired. "I need some rare plants for my potions."

"I'll be leaving tomorrow, mother. I have a message for the queen from a Japanese friend of hers."

The prince, having overheard this conversation, emerged from his corner, to everyone's surprise. Even the old woman had forgotten all about him!

"Oh, please take me with you, East Wind" he begged. "I've been traveling the mountains and the forests for so long, looking for the Garden of Paradise."

The mother of the winds told him that the garden was very far away indeed and that the journey there was a grueling one. But the young man was adamant and said that he was prepared to sacrifice everything, to undergo any ordeal, just to see it.

"Very well! Tomorrow morning, very early, you can climb on my back and I will take you there," East Wind agreed.

When the prince opened his eyes the next morning, he was already perched on the East Wind's shoulders. His fantastic journey had begun!

After they had flown above the clouds for a long long time, East Wind and the prince flew down to earth and into a very dark grotto. Eventually, they reached a silver river, the water of which shimmered with countless golden fish.

"The Garden of Paradise lies beyond this river," explained East Wind.

They crossed over a magnificent marble bridge and entered a garden full of beautiful, sweet-smelling plants and flowers.

Multicolored birds were singing lovely melodies.

The prince was gazing wide-eyed at all these incredible sights when, suddenly, a young woman wearing a dress of rich brocade came up to them, smiling.

"Welcome to the Garden of Paradise!" she said.

East Wind bowed low and kissed her hand and delivered the message he had brought her from Japan, then he introduced the prince, telling her of his great desire to visit her kingdom.

The young woman was the queen of the garden. She was

divinely beautiful and the long hair falling gracefully across her shoulders seemed to shine like spun gold.

She took the young man's hand and led him into her glass palace. She took him through several spacious rooms with transparent crystal walls into a high spacious hall at the center of which stood a majestic tree with jewel-encrusted leaves. They glittered and sparkled like fire and the golden fruit of the tree shone as brightly as the rays of the sun.

At the foot of the tree flowed a spring, its clear water ran with a sound like sweet music.

"These are the Tree of Knowledge and the Spring of Wisdom," the queen explained. "No stranger to the country may take advantage of their gifts. You may stay here for as long as you like, but you are forbidden to so much as touch a leaf of the tree or a single drop of the water from the spring. If you were to disobey this command, the Garden of Paradise would disappear under the earth, the desert wind would whistle wildly around you, and a freezing rain destroy you."

"I would not wish to displease you in any way, and I could wish for no greater happiness than to spend the rest of my life at your side," replied the prince, who was already half in love with the queen.

"Consider well, it will not be easy. You can still change your mind and go back with East Wind."

"I am staying here with you!"

"Well then, let us go to the banquet hall where a great feast has been prepared in your honor."

In the great hall, there was a chorus of beautiful girls who sang to the accompaniment of rippling harps, while pretty dancing girls swayed and spun with their veils floating around them like pale mist.

The prince was enchanted. He had never seen such a wonderful spectacle or such divine beauty.

Late that night, East Wind said goodbye to the queen, promising to return again soon. He left, taking with him the rare herbs his mother had asked him to bring her.

The queen and the prince walked for a little while longer among the flowers and jewels of the palace, then the queen took her leave, for she was very tired. She opened a little door in the trunk of the Tree of Knowledge and all at once she was gone, leaving the young man alone.

With a single bound, he ran to follow her and tried to force the door open. There was a long deafening roll of thunder. With a frightful crashing roar, the Garden of Paradise disappeared into the ground forever. Suddenly the prince was seized by an icy cold wind and fell lifeless to the ground.

Then a freezing rain cut right through to his bones. He barely had the strength to open his eyes, but when he did, he realized that he was lying in the grotto of the mother of the winds. The fire had gone out. It was terribly cold.

The mother of the winds was not there. At his side, the queen of the Garden of Paradise was waiting for him to awaken. Then she said to him,

"You have only your own curiosity to blame for your loss! Go back to your people now, for they need you, and govern them wisely. When you have accomplished your mission there, I shall return to take you to the Garden of Paradise."

AUTHOR INDEX

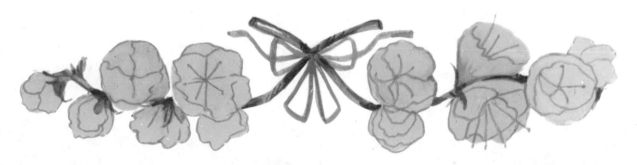

THE BROTHERS GRIMM

CHARLES PERRAULT